Chip had had no idea that farming was such hard work. He was very tired. Now it was time for him to pack his suitcase and go back to the city.

"Packity pack. Off so soon, my boy?" said Farmer Chundo.

"Good-bye, Farmer Chundo.
Good-bye, Batty and Crooky.

I've learned a lot about farming. Thank you."

"Good-bye, Chip. Come back soon," said Batty.

"Yes, come back soon," said Crooky.

Two days later, the McDoubles received, along with some bills, a letter from Chip. It read:

Dear Batty and Crooky and Farmer Chundo,

Thank you for letting me visit you on your farm. There's a lot more to farming than I realized. My uncle Dizzie has given me a job at his nightclub. Please come visit me in the city if you're not too busy with farm chores.

Yours truly,
Chip

P.S. How's the garden? Any weeds? Don't forget to water . . . or whatever.

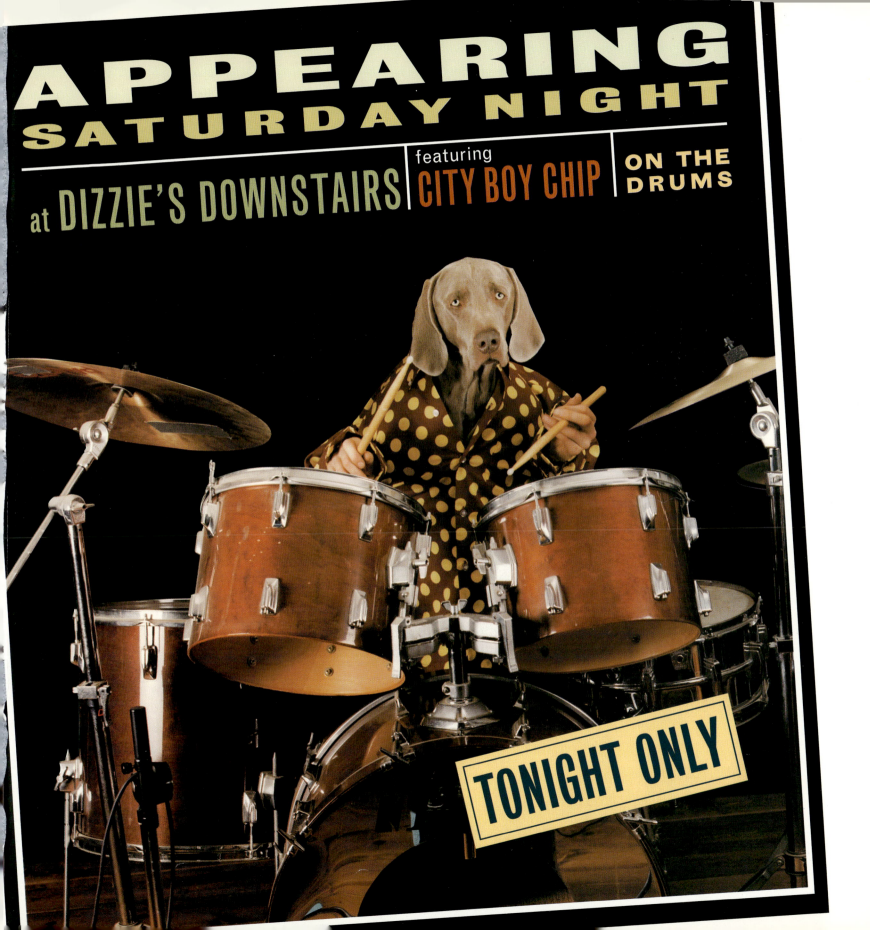

For information address
Hyperion Books for Children, 114 Fifth Avenue, New York, New York 10011-5690

First Edition
1 3 5 7 9 10 8 6 4 2

Library of Congress Cataloging-in-Publication Data

Wegman, William.
[Farm days]
William Wegman's farm days: or how Chip learnt an important lesson on the farm,
or a day in the country, or hip Chip's trip, or farmer boy.
p.   cm.
Summary: Chip, a city dog, goes to visit his country cousins to learn all about farming.
ISBN 0-7868-0216-2 (trade) — ISBN 0-7868-2286-4 (lib. bdg.)
[1. Dogs—Fiction. 2. Farm life—Fiction.] I. Title.
PZ7.W4234Wi 1997
[E]—dc20
96-35922

DESIGN: DRENTTEL DOYLE PARTNERS

This book is set in Bureau Grotesque, Century Oldstyle, Frutiger, Grotesque, Officina Sans, and Rockwell.

Acknowledgments

WITH THANKS TO:

Jason Burch, Christine Burgin, David Deutsch, Drenttel Doyle Partners, Arnaldo Hernandez,
Julie Hindley, J & J Mill Creek Farm, Eric Jeffreys, Love Apple Orchard, Asia Linn,
Mr. & Mrs. McCagg, Dave McMillan, The Pace/MacGill Gallery, Howard Reeves,
Victoria Sambonaris, Tonnie Sauca, Katleen Sterck, and Pam Wegman.

*We would especially like to thank Michael Schrom and
Caroline Brackenridge at Old Mill Farm.*

llama llama
holiday drama

Anna Dewdney

SCHOLASTIC INC.
New York Toronto London Auckland
Sydney Mexico City New Delhi Hong Kong

For the Luhrmann family

ISBN 978-0-545-27947-5

12 11 10 9 8 7 6 5 4 3 2 1   PHX   11 12 13 14 15 16/0

Printed in the U.S.A.

First Scholastic printing, February 2011

Set in ITC Quorum

Llama Llama holidays.
Jingle music. Lights ablaze.

Sparkly candles. Yummy bread.
Dress-up clothes in green and red.

How long till that special date?

ONLY 15 MORE SHOPPING DAYS!

Llama Llama has to **wait.**

Llama Llama holidays.
Ads and signs and store displays.

ONLY 12 MORE
SHOPPING DAYS!

Fluffy snow and funny elves.
Goodies piled high on shelves.

Just **how many** days to go?
Llama Llama wants to know.

Time to buy and
search and shop.

Mama carries.   Llama drops.

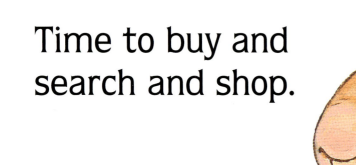

Buy a friend a rubber duck?
Pirate ship or tractor truck?
Wooden blocks or
building set?

HOLIDAY SALE!

What will Llama Llama get?

Llama Llama holidays.
Hustle bustle.
Cooking craze.
Measure sugar.
Roll the dough.
Ten more batches
left to go. . . .

How many more days, again?
The special day
is coming **when?**

Make a great big batch for school!
Take more cookies out to cool.

Add some sprinkles. Almost done. . . .
Teacher gets the fancy one.

No more cookies left to bake!

Llama Llama tummy-ache.

School has dreidels, songs, and bells.
Big red ribbons, woodsy smells.

Draw a snowman. Make a star.
Decorate a candle jar.

I am a Llama

Are there many days to go? Llama time is going **s l o w . . . .**

Mama needs a present, too!
Get some sparkles, sticks, and glue.

Roll it up and wrap it how?
Llama wants to give it **now!**

Llama Llama holidays.
Unpack stockings.
Unwrap trays.

Shiny silver.
Fancy plates.

Llama Llama
waits, waits, **waits.**

Cut out snowflakes.
Tape them up.
Pour some eggnog in a cup.

Oops . . . it's yucky on
the floor.

Llama Llama waits
some more.

Stringing lights is not much fun.
How come Mama isn't done?
Is the big day coming soon?
Llama Llama starts to swoon....

All this waiting for **one day?**

Time for presents **RIGHT AWAY!**

Too much music, too much fluff!
Too much making, too much stuff!

Too much **everything** for Llama . . .

Llama Llama, HOLIDRAMA!

Come and listen, little Llama.
Have a cuddle with your mama.

Sometimes we should take a rest
and hold the ones we love the best.

Wishing, waiting, wanting things . . .
we forget what this time brings.

Gifts are nice,
but there's another—
the true gift is
we have each other.

Llama Llama, warm and snug,
gives a kiss and gets a hug,
snuggles close with Mama Llama. . . .

Happy holidays for Llama.